E
ICH   Ichikawa, Satomi
         Nora's roses

$14.95

DATE			

C2

BAKER & TAYLOR BOOKS

NORA'S ROSES

To my grandmother
with memories of my childhood

NORA'S ROSES

Satomi Ichikawa

PHILOMEL BOOKS

Nora could not stop blowing her nose; her eyes were watery. It was a good thing that Teddy the bear, Maggie the doll, and Kiki the dog could stay with her. At least they kept her company. Even so, it had been more than a week!

What could be more boring than this? Nora thought.

Then Teddy, who was a bit bored, too, pulled the curtain open.

Outside the roses were in full bloom.

Just then, Great Aunt Betty came
along. She was on her way to a bridge
party.

"I'll just take one," she said. "It will
make such a nice present for my friends."
And she picked a rose.

It wasn't long before John and Paul came by.

"Nora, come and play!" John called, but the roses smelled so good, Paul picked one.

Roger was on his way to a concert
when he smelled the roses' sweet scent.
"I'll just take one for my button-
hole," he said, and he did.

Roger had not been gone long, when
the carpenter, Peter, and his daughter,
Juliet, came along.

"That is just the color I want for
your room, Juliet," he said, and he
took a rose to remember.

A boy on roller skates flew past and picked a rose as he went.

Even Ralph, from across the street, came along and sniffed the roses. Well, thought Nora, I suppose you want a rose, too.

Achoo! Nora blew her nose again. Then she saw three friends, Peggy, Sara, and Vera.

"Can't you come to our tea party, Nora?" Peggy said. "What a pity."

Vera took a rose to the tea party.
But Nora stayed at home.

Her roses had gone to a bridge party, a concert, and a tea party, but Nora couldn't go anywhere.

"Oh, I wish I could have gone," Nora thought.

She was settling into her quilts, when
she heard *tap, tap, tap*.

Someone was knocking on the window.

"Oh, dear," Nora said. "It's my roses! They're going somewhere."

"We're going to a party. Would you like to come?"

"Jump into a rose, and join us," one flower said.

And that is what Nora, Maggie, and Kiki did—they jumped into the roses.

"Hurry up, Teddy," Nora called.

And the four friends went to a rose concert,
and a dancing party of roses.

Then they had delicious cake, Teddy's favorite, with rose tea and rose candy. They were just enjoying the wonderful tea party when it turned unexpectedly into a bridge party.

They were just about to have soup and rose petal sandwiches at the bridge party, when suddenly someone shouted, "Nora, Nora, look!"

A monster was at the window!
Maggie, Teddy, and Kiki were
upset about that.

The monster was only Buttercup, the neighbor's cow. But she was eating Nora's roses!

"Shoo!" the four friends shouted all at once. "Away from our roses!" And Nora threw everything she could find to scare off the cow.

"Greedy old Buttercup," Nora mumbled. Kiki was tired from barking, and poor Teddy had been thrown at the "monster" and was a bit tired himself.

Nora looked out. There was only
one rose left.

Oh, Nora wanted to keep that last rose. But how? Could she press it in a book? Could she hang it in the kitchen to dry it? Perhaps she could make potpourri? Or perfume? Teddy, Kiki, and Maggie all helped Nora think.

"I know what I'll do," Nora finally said right out loud. "I'll make a picture."

And that is what Nora did. She drew the rose, and kept it forever.

English translation copyright © 1993 by Philomel Books. Original edition copyright © 1991 by Satomi Ichikawa. First American edition published in 1993 by Philomel Books, a division of The Putnam & Grosset Group, 200 Madison Avenue, New York, NY 10016. Originally published in Japanese in 1991 by Kaisei-Sha Publishing Co., Ltd., Tokyo, under the title *Bara ga saita*. English translation rights arranged with Kaisei-Sha Publishing Co., Ltd., through Japan Foreign-Rights Centre. All rights reserved. This book, or parts thereof, may not be reproduced in any form without permission in writing from the publisher. Published simultaneously in Canada. Printed in Hong Kong by South China Printing Co. (1988), Ltd. Book design by Jean Weiss. The text is set in Baskerville.

The artist used watercolor paints to create the art for this book. It was then scanned by laser and separated into four colors, for reproduction on sheetfed offset printing presses.

Library of Congress Cataloging-in-Publication Data. Ichikawa, Satomi. Nora's roses / by Satomi Ichikawa. p. cm. Summary: After watching other people pick and carry off most of her roses while she is sick in bed, Nora has a special dream involving the flowers. [1. Roses—Fiction. 2. Sick—Fiction. 3. Dreams—Fiction.] I. Title. PZ7.I16Ns 1993 [E]—dc20 91-46145 CIP AC ISBN 0-399-21968-4

1 3 5 7 9 10 8 6 4 2

First Impression